MY MAGIC GARDEN

A Meditation Guide for Children

Ilse Klipper

Pathways Press,
Palo Alto, California

Photographs by Joan Kavanau

Illustrations by Maureen Green, Jennifer Heath, Mark Mc. Auliffe, Tammy Sanford, and Tarah Smith

My Magic Garden

2nd Printing March 1981
Printed in the United States of America

ISBN 0-9605022-0-3

Pathways Press
P.O. Box 11196-A
Palo Alto, California 94306

To my beloved Baba.

ACKNOWLEDGMENTS

My grateful thanks go to my teacher, Ram Butler, whose correspondence course has been my daily guide for the past four years.

Appreciation to Karen Burbank for her painstaking efforts and assistance in making this book a reality.

Special thanks to Eleanor Perkins, to my daughter Francoise Netter, to my young student Mark McAuliffe, and to Janaia Donaldson for their valuable comments after reviewing this book.

CONTENTS

AN INVITATION TO PARENTS

Although this book is written so that a child can easily follow all the activities by himself or herself, I invite you to participate with them. Any activity in which a parent shares time with his or her child makes that activity twice as precious to the child. There is an added possibility that you may see that the joy and peace your child finds in these activities are also available to you! For it is true that we find true happiness with the heart of a child.

If you are unable to accept this invitation wholeheartedly, I request your beginning supervision of the breathing exercises because they are so basic to learning how to relax.

If your child has any breathing related problems, please check with your physician before your child begins the deep breathing exercises.

I thank you for giving this special gift to one you love.

INTRODUCTION

Dear Friend,

With great love and respect, I invite you to join me in *My Magic Garden.*

My name is Prabha. In Sanskrit, the ancient language of India, my name means "radiant light." I have shared my love and the joy of meditation with many young people like yourself. Some of my young friends thought it would be fun to share these experiences with you in a book.

This book can be like your best friend. The more you see your friends, the more you enjoy and understand them. *My Magic Garden* can become your friend for a long, long time. Every time you read it you will discover something new. The more you read it and do the same things over and over, the more you will enjoy it. As you work with this book over and over, the more you will come to understand yourself and, most of all, to love yourself.

You will find that this book is quite different from other books you have read. A book is usually read for fun or for learning about something. This book gives you the chance to feel and to do what you are reading about. The best way to really believe something is to find out about it for yourself. You cannot really know how an apple tastes until you have eaten one. You can't really know about something only by looking at it or reading about it. The best way to know just about anything is by trying it for yourself.

This book can become an exciting new experience for you. Take time each day to join me in a quiet room or in a place where you feel most comfortable. If you follow what I am doing, you may soon notice a change in how you feel about yourself and others. Everyday from now on can become a happy surprise. This book is divided into seven parts or seven days. It is best to read only one day at a time. On each day I answer questions asked by young students like yourself. Many of those questions could relate to things happening to you. After the questions and answers, I teach some exercises that can help to relax your body and make it feel good. I will then guide your mind to think about a beautiful place called the Magic Garden. "Taking a walk" through the Magic Garden will relax your mind and give you happy feelings.

I would very much like to hear from you. If you have any questions that you don't find answers to in *My Magic Garden*, please write to me at Pathways Press. The address can be found at the bottom of page ii. For a personal answer to your question, please include a stamped envelope with your name and address written on it. I will try to answer you as soon as possible. Some of your questions may even be answered in the next volume of *My Magic Garden*.

With much love,
Prabha

DAY ONE

WHO AM I? WHO ARE YOU?

Hello, dear friend! Welcome to Day One. Today you will meet a wonderful person. You will become acquainted with that person and will discover things you never before noticed. Do you know who that person is? Yes, you guessed right. That beautiful person is you!

Let me help you get to know yourself. Look into a mirror. What do you see? Look at your eyes and eyebrows. Did you ever notice the kind look and the bright color in your eyes? Smile at yourself. That was only a little smile! Now try a very big smile. That is much better. See how great you look! Now look at your hair. What a perfect color! Touch it and run your fingers through it. Gently rub your head with your fingers. That feels good, doesn't it.

Close your eyes. Feel your face with both hands. Move your fingers over every part of your face very slowly and gently. Begin by moving over your forehead and onto your eyes. Now move over your nose, over your ears, down over your cheeks, and onto your mouth. Feel your lips and your chin. How good it feels to touch all these parts of your face. You will be surprised to find how this little bit of time spent with yourself can make you feel so good.

Now get to know the rest of your body. Look at your hands. Watch your fingers as you move them in many different directions. You can do many things with your hands. Aren't they amazing! Look in the mirror and watch your body move. Watch how your chest and stomach move while you breathe in and out. Can you see other parts of your body moving? Your body is such a great and amazing machine. Do you give it enough attention or do you take your body for granted? No wonder it hurts and aches from time to time. These aches remind you to give it more attention and to appreciate it a little more.

Now look at your legs. Try out different ways of moving them. Bend your knees. Isn't it wonderful to be able to move them so easily? Next, take off your shoes. ALWAYS TAKE OFF YOUR SHOES WHILE DOING EXERCISES AND MEDITATION. It feels more comfortable to have them off. Now sit down and rub one toe at a time with your thumb. Rub your feet, too. If it feels good, you can practice rubbing whenever you are watching television or have nothing else to do.

Now that you have begun to know your body you might want to look at it more often. It is your very own body. How it grows and develops depends on how well you take care of it.

QUESTIONS AND ANSWERS

Who Am I?

You are a perfect person filled with light, love, joy, and peace. You can learn how to discover these beautiful treasures locked deep within you. You must first learn to know who you are.

Everything that happens in your life has the purpose of teaching you something about yourself. That is called learning a lesson. You also learn lessons in school. There you learn how to read, write, count, spell, and other wonderful things. These lessons are not taught to you as punishment or to make your life difficult. These are things you must know in order to get along in life. Outside of school, you also have experiences that can be called lessons because they teach you something new about yourself. In this book I hope to teach you many different lessons. I especially want to show you how to use those lessons to bring you closer to your inner Self. You will be surprised, as you read through Day Two, to find that your inner Self is in the center of all those treasures which I have called light, love, joy, and peace.

Who Are You?

I am like you! I am a perfect person who is able to learn my lessons. The only difference between you and me, or everyone else, is that each of us has different lessons to learn. That is why each of us behaves differently from one another. But within, we are like one another.

What Lesson Must I Learn?

An important lesson you must learn is how to know who you really are. You come to know who you are by knowing your inner Self. Once you know your inner Self, you can enjoy every moment of your life. Then whatever you do can be a good experience and even fun.

Can Boring Work Like Doing Homework Or Cleaning Up A Messy Room Be Fun?

Yes. Everything you do all day long can be fun once you learn how to look within yourself.

How Can I Learn To Know Myself?

You can know by learning how to become very still. When you are very quiet you can "listen" to what is going on within yourself. When you learn to "listen" to what is going on within yourself, you can learn a lot about your own feelings.

What Do I Need To Know About Myself?

That you are perfect the way you are. You may be tall or short and light or heavy. The way your body looks may be just another lesson for you to learn. For example, if you are heavier than most of your friends, you may want to change that and learn to discipline yourself. Discipline means self-control. You need to do regular exercises and watch how much food you eat. That takes discipline but it will help you to learn the lesson of responsibility.

Why Is It Important For Me To Be Responsible?

When you learn to be responsible for yourself and for what happens to you, you will feel good about yourself. When you become responsible, you will no longer have to blame your parents, brothers, sisters, friends, or teachers for unpleasant

4

things that happen to you. For example, if you get a low grade on a test, do not blame your teacher. Accept the fact that you received the grade you earned. When you can accept that good grades come with your best effort, you will have learned something about responsibility. When you are responsible you will know that if you want good grades you will have to give attention to your studies and do your work. The more you take responsibility for your actions, the better you will feel about yourself.

How Can I See The Beauty Inside Myself?

You will come to see it as you practice with this book every day. In the beginning, it may be difficult to take the time for it. But once you see that this book can help your days to be more fun, you may want to work with it more and more. There is so much to do and talk about. Let us begin with the exercises.

EXERCISES

I will teach you some exercises that will help you to relax your body. Before you can relax your mind it is necessary to learn how to relax your body. Your body and mind work together. When your body feels good and is relaxed, it will be much easier for your mind to also feel good and relaxed.

On this first day, you will practice stretching exercises. Each day I will share different exercises with you. If you read the directions and look at the pictures as you go along, you will soon find that you can easily do the exercises.

In my group I play soft background music for the exercises and Magic Garden "Walk". The music I like is on a cassette tape and is called *A Soundtrack For Everyone—Spectrum Suite.* (If you would like to use this music, look for it on record or tape at your local music store. If you can't find it at the store, you can order a record or tape from Halpern Sound, 620 Taylor Way #14, Belmont, Ca. 94002, or telephone (415) 592-4900.)

For both the exercises and Magic Garden "Walk" it is very important that you find a quiet place where you won't be disturbed. You should try to set aside at least twenty minutes for the exercises and the "walk." A good time might be in the morning if you can get up earlier than you usually do. Or, you might want to save some time in the evening before going to bed. If there are some days in which you can spare only five or ten minutes, that will help you too. The more time you take for doing the exercises, the better you will feel.

SOME OF THE EXERCISES YOU WILL LEARN ARE STRETCHING EXERCISES. IT IS VERY IMPORTANT THAT YOU STRETCH ONLY AS HIGH AS IT FEELS GOOD TO YOU. Do not exercise in a way that will hurt you as you do it. Make sure that you do all the exercises very slowly.

Exercise 1: "Stretching Up"

Stand straight with both feet slightly apart. Make sure your back is straight. Pull your stomach in.

Raise both arms toward the ceiling.

Stretch your right arm, then stretch your left arm. Keep stretching one arm at a time. Count twenty stretches all together.

Now bring your arms down slowly and shake your hands a few times.

Exercise 2: "Stretching With Folded Hands"

Stand with both feet slightly apart.

Raise both arms toward the ceiling.

Fold your hands tightly together and stretch your arms up as high as you can. Count slowly to ten.

Now bend your upper body to the right (look at picture) and stretch as far as you can. Hold your body in this way and count to ten.

Now, bend your upper body to the left and stretch as far as you can. Again hold your body in this way and count to ten.

Bring your arms back above your head. Unfold your hands and slowly drop your arms down to your sides.

Shake your hands a few more times.

Deep Breathing: Place your hands close to your body and take a deep breath, breathing in deeply through your nose with your mouth closed. Hold your breath as you count to five. Now let the breath out slowly through your mouth as if you were blowing out a candle.

Exercise 3: "Stretching Down"

Stand up straight with your feet apart and stretch your arms as high as you can.

Bring your stretched arms down in front of your right foot and count slowly to ten. With each count, gently bounce up and bounce down, almost to the floor. Touch the floor with your fingertips.

Then, while you are still bending down, bring your body and arms between your legs and touch the floor lightly with your fingertips.

Let your arms hang loose like a puppet as you count to ten.

Now bring your body and arms in front of your left foot and gently bounce up and down to the count of ten.

Raise your arms back above your head, slowly bring them down, and shake both hands.

Shake each foot one at a time and take another deep breath.

A "WALK" INTO YOUR MAGIC GARDEN

Now that your body is relaxed, you can "walk" into your Magic Garden to relax your mind and feel happy feelings. First you must learn how to get into your Magic Garden. Sit crosslegged on the floor or in a comfortable chair. You may even lie on the floor if that is comfortable for you. Make sure that your back is straight and place your hands to your side.

Take a deep breath through your nose while counting to four. Hold your breath and count to four. Then count to eight while letting it out slowly through your mouth. Take two more deep breaths in the same way. Make a fist with each hand and squeeze them as hard as you can. Clench your teeth and tighten up your whole body for a quick moment. Then loosen your body, flop, like a Raggedy Ann doll.

Now you will be loosening (sometimes called relaxing) all of your body, part by part. Wiggle your toes to loosen them and think about your feet as you feel them relaxing. Relax your legs by thinking about them as loose. Can you feel your legs relaxing all the way up to your hips? Think about your hands and your arms all the way up to your shoulders as relaxed and feeling good. As you think about relaxing your stomach and then your chest, feel yourself breathing in and out. Then relax the lower part and the upper part of your back. Now can you think and feel your neck as completely relaxed? Also think about every part of your face and feel your chin, your lips, your cheeks, your eyes, your forehead, and even the top of your head as you relax each of them.

Now relax your mind. You can do this by thinking hard about what you are doing just now. Don't be bothered if other thoughts come to your mind. Just "tell" the thoughts you will think about them later.

Very shortly you will be inside of your Magic Garden. To "walk" through it and to "see" everything that is there, it is good to start out with a guide. You will find the guide for the Magic Garden "Walk" on page 13. There are three different ways to use it. You choose the one that works best for you.

1. You can have someone read the Magic Garden "Walk" to you in a very slow and soft voice. You may want to have some soft music in the background so that you won't be bothered by

outside noises. While it is being read to you, close your eyes and place your hands next to you with palms up.

2. You can record the guide on a tape. Read the guide in a very slow and soft voice. Then play the tape and listen to it with your eyes closed and your hands, with palms up, next to you.

3. You can read the part over a few times until you know it quite well. Then, think it in your mind while you sit or lie down with your eyes closed and your hands, with palms up, next to you.

A GUIDE FOR THE MAGIC GARDEN "WALK"

You are walking on a beautiful road. You are carrying several bags of seed, some plants, and tools. Soon you reach a fence. It has a locked gate. You reach into your pocket for your golden key. Open the gate with your key. You will see some land that is now all yours. You will use this piece of land to make your Magic Garden. If you want to make a lawn, sow some grass seed. Or, plant some flowers and other things you want to grow. Place anything else you might like into your garden. Spend some time arranging your garden the way you want it to look. Dig into the ground and water it. (A few moments of silence.) Some time has now gone by. Do you see the flowers, grass, and plants growing? Think more about your garden and notice that happy feeling within yourself. This is a place that you have created. This garden can have everything in it you want it to have. Anything that is special to you can be placed here. This garden is yours and only yours. (A few minutes of silence.) Whenever you are ready to leave, close the gate behind you and lock it with your golden key. Place the key in your pocket.

You may enter your Magic Garden anytime that you wish. You only need about ten minutes of time and a quiet place. Your garden can be wherever you are and it can be whatever you would like it to be. Now it is time to bring your own thoughts back, to close your palms, and to very slowly open your eyes. Stay still for a few moments so that your body and your mind can slowly become active after this quiet time.

If you had trouble picturing your garden today, try it again tomorrow. If you could see your garden clearly today, then begin drawing a picture of your Magic Garden on the next page. You can color in the sky but do not place any clouds or stars in it. It is easy to draw your Magic Garden if you can remember all of its details. The Magic Garden is to be planted only one time. Whenever you reread Day One, all that you need to do is look at your Magic Garden picture before you close your eyes. After doing the deep breathing exercises and relaxing, go directly to your Magic Garden and do exactly what you feel like doing there on that day.

I enjoyed sharing this day with you and look forward to being with you tomorrow.

Draw your Magic Garden here. Save the space above the dotted line for the sky which you will work with on Day Six.

- -

DAY TWO

WHAT IS MEDITATION?

Hello, special friend! It is good to meet with you again. Today, I will answer some questions about meditation (med-i-ta-tion). It is a word that is used quite often these days. For many, it is a difficult word to understand. But I will help you understand it and show you how useful the meditation activity can be.

QUESTIONS AND ANSWERS

What Is Meditation?

Meditation is an activity in which you direct all your thoughts and attention to one main idea so that you can understand that idea deeply. Most people meditate at some time during the day. For example, in school, you are meditating whenever you concentrate ONLY on that which your teacher is teaching at that moment. You are also meditating whenever you draw a picture or play an instrument and become completely absorbed in what you are doing. Meditation is simply giving all of your attention to whatever you are doing at a certain moment. This kind of meditation is concentration on something that can be seen, heard, or touched. In Yoga (which I will tell you about), meditation means concentrating or directing your thoughts to your inner Self. So you see, you have been meditating on many things at different times and probably didn't even know it as meditation.

What Does Yoga Mean?

Yoga means union or being at one with one's self. You feel very peaceful when you are at one with yourself. Whenever your mind and your body feel good you will be very much at peace. You may wonder how your mind and body can be helped to feel good. Well, your mind feels good when it thinks quiet or happy thoughts. You can make your mind quiet through Yoga meditation. Your body feels good when it is relaxed. You can make your body relaxed through Yoga exercises.

What Is My Inner Self?

Your inner Self is your inner awareness. It is deep within you. You cannot see it as you can see your outer self, but you can be in touch with your inner Self when your mind is very quiet.

Your inner Self is the source of all your good feelings such as joy, love and happiness.

What Can Meditation Do For Me?

It can quiet your mind. When your mind is quiet, you will be better able to do whatever it is you need to do. And, when your mind is still, you will discover wonderful feelings inside yourself.

Why Is Meditation Important?

Meditation, or concentration, is important in your daily life because without it, it is not easy to become good at what you do. When you don't do your best work, you may become upset and angry or even jealous of others who do well.

How Can I Learn To Concentrate On My Work?

You can learn if you practice meditating every day. This will train your mind to become quiet, giving you total peace and total stillness within. Once you discover this peaceful feeling within yourself, you will be able to use it whenever you have to concentrate on your work. If you have difficulty concentrating on what you are doing, take a few deep breaths to calm your mind. Look again at Exercise 2 in Day One to help you deep breathe.

*Can I Practice Meditation While "Walking" Through My
Magic Garden?*

Yes, it is a very good way to begin practicing meditation. But there are also many other ways to meditate. You can concentrate on your breathing or repeat a mantra (man-tra). A mantra is one or more words that make a special sound movement when you speak them. Another way is to think of your heart as a white light. It is best to follow just one way until you feel very comfortable with it.

How Can Meditation Help Me?

One of the best ways to find happiness, love, and joy is through meditation. Your heart is like a bright white light. Your heart is filled with many wonderful feelings. You can only feel these feelings of love, peace, happiness, and joy when you are quiet and your mind is still. All day long you are so busy with your outside world that you forget about the magic within. Sometimes you may even forget to notice beautiful things like the song of a bird or a beautiful flower.

Meditation can train your mind to look for things that make you feel good instead of things that bother you. It can also help to train your mind for learning things you want to learn. Meditation can also help you to enjoy your schoolwork. Meditation can even reach in and bring out your inner magic. You will experience many happy changes as you learn to meditate.

EXERCISES

Remember to wear comfortable clothes without belts or tight bands and to remove your shoes whenever you exercise. You may want to turn on background music for exercising and for your Magic Garden "Walk". Do not allow yourself to be disturbed during your exercise and relaxation period.

Exercise 1: "The Tree"

This exercise is very good for quieting your mind and for learning concentration.

Stand firm on both legs.

Find a small part of an object or wall spot straight ahead of you and look at it.

Very slowly move your right foot up as high as you can against your left leg.

Lift both arms up and place your hands together (check the picture).

Now stand still and look straight ahead at the small part or spot. Keep your mind on that spot and do not think about anything else. Very slowly count to ten.

Gently let your hands and leg down.

Now do the same with your left leg but try to hold the position longer this time.

With practice, you will be able to hold a leg to the count of thirty, forty, or even sixty. Try to feel very calm and quiet when you do this exercise.

Now shake each hand and each foot one at a time.

Exercise 2: "Chest Expansion"

This exercise will help you to develop your chest and lungs. It will also help you to have a better posture.

Stand with your arms at your side and feet slightly apart. Pull in your stomach and straighten your back.

Slowly raise your arms until they are even with your shoulders. Bend your elbows until both of your hands touch each other (look at picture A).

Slowly stretch your arms straight our before you (picture B).

Now bring them backward as far as possible.

Drop your arms behind your back and join your hands together. Hold your body straight and push out your chest.

With your joined hands still behind you, raise them as high as possible.

Push your upper body and head backwards so that you can see the ceiling (picture C).

Hold this position while slowly counting to five.

Now, from your waist, bend forward and gently bring up your arms and joined hands as high as you can.

Do not bend your knees. Continue to bend forward from your waist until your head is hanging straight down and your hands are reaching as high above you as possible. (Do not pull your arms too hard.)

Hold this position while counting to ten (picture D).

Slowly come back up to a straight standing position.

Loosen your hands and shake them.

Take a deep breath. Repeat the "Chest Expansion" exercise one more time.

A

B

C

D

Exercise 3: "Stretch Down" (holding the lower part of your leg)

Stand straight. Place your feet as far apart as feels comfortable for you.

Raise both arms with your palms facing one another.

Stretch up as high as it feels good for you.

Now bend down and bring both hands down to your left foot (look at the picture).

Grab your lower leg with both hands while keeping both legs straight.

Bend your arms and gently bring your head as close to your leg as is possible. Bring your head only as far as it feels comfortable to do, but don't force it.

Hold this position and count to ten.

Now come up slowly. Drag both hands along your leg as you come upward.

When your hands reach your hip, let them drop next to you.

Take a deep breath.

Stand straight and again place your feet apart.

Raise both arms with your palms facing one another and stretch upward.

Repeat this exercise but grab your right leg instead of your left.

After you finish this exercise, first shake both hands and then shake your left and your right foot.

Take a deep breath through your nose and while slowly breathing out, say the long sound of "o".

Repeat the "Stretch Down" exercise for both your left and right leg.

A "WALK" INTO YOUR MAGIC GARDEN

Now that you are relaxed and calm, explore your Magic Garden. Keep the music on at a very low volume. Find a comfortable position, sitting either in a chair or on the floor with legs crossed. You may want to lie flat on the floor if it feels better for you.

As you did on Day One, take a deep breath through your nose while counting to four. Hold your breath as you count to four. Slowly let your breath out through your mouth while counting to eight. Repeat this deep breathing exercise two more times.

With your hands close to you, make a fist with each hand and squeeze them as hard as you can. Now tighten up your whole body including your muscles in your feet, in your legs, your hands, arms, stomach, chest, and in your back. Tighten your back, the back of your head, your face, your mouth, your nose, and squeeze your eyes shut. Now let your whole body loosen, flop, like a Raggedy Ann doll. Think about every part of your body to make sure that all muscles are completely relaxed.

Now it is time to relax your mind. Only concentrate on what you are doing and if other thoughts come into your mind, gently "tell" them they will be taken care of later. Close your eyes and slowly place your hands, with palms up, next to you.

Picture yourself walking along the road leading to your Magic Garden. You are at the gate so take your key out of your pocket and open it. You are now in your garden so close the gate behind you. Take a look around and enjoy what you have created. Is there anything you need to do in your garden? Do the grass and flowers need to be watered? Do the birds need some food? Just take the time and do whatever needs to be done. (A few moments of silence.) Do the things in your garden that you really enjoy doing. Feel that working in your garden is fun and like play. You alone made your garden so only you can decide what you want to do in it. (A few moments of silence.)

Now it's time to explore your garden. Walk along the path and find a place to sit down to rest and look around. It is so beautiful and peaceful. As you get up, you see something under a garden rock. As you lift the rock, you can't believe what you see. There is the answer to something you always wanted to know. As you bend down to look a little closer, a little voice whispers in your ear saying, "This is a secret only you can know. You are free to come here every day and learn more about it. All you need to do is lift this rock and look, feel, and listen. This secret will always be yours. Now place the rock back where it belongs." (A few moments of silence.)

Now it is about time to leave your Magic Garden. Would you like to bend down and smell some of the beautiful flowers? Perhaps you would like to pick a few flowers to take home with you. (A moment of silence.) Walk along the path to the gate. Lock the gate with your key as you leave and place your key in your pocket.

Now it is time to bring your thoughts back, to close your palms, and to slowly open your eyes. Stay still for a few moments.

If you wish, you can do your meditation at night in bed and then go right off to sleep. Have a good night's sleep and I will be with you tomorrow.

DAY THREE

WHAT ARE DREAMS?

Hello, my friend! After three days together I have come to feel very close to you. Today I am going to tell you about dreams. You usually dream while you sleep. Some dreams you remember and some dreams you forget. Some dreams are exciting and other dreams are frightening. Let me help you understand your dreams.

QUESTIONS AND ANSWERS

What Are Dreams?

   Dreams are messages received from your inner Self.

What Do Dreams Tell?

   Dreams can tell you about your feelings, your fears, and your wishes.

Why Do I Dream?

   You dream to learn lessons about yourself, to help you understand yourself better. Sometimes you do things that hurt you and dreams can show you how to change that.

How Can I Learn From My Dreams?

   You can learn from dreams by giving more attention to them. They can get your attention because they come "dressed up" or "in costume." If, for example, you wear a costume in a play or at Halloween; others are likely to give attention to you. The same is true with dreams. Because they are so crazily "dressed" they can be remembered. If the dreams appeared as real life, you would not give much attention to them. Some of the messages or the lessons to be learned can come to you as well in your dreams as when you are awake, only in a different "costume." Messages or lessons will return again and again until you understand and learn from them.

How Can I Learn To Understand My Dreams?

You can understand your dream by carefully looking at each part of it. Each person in your dream usually takes the place of you. Words will have different meanings. Dreaming about rain or water usually is telling you something about your emotions or feelings. Climbing a hill could mean something is hard for you to do. Colors and numbers also have different meanings. It will take a little time to figure out your dreams, but continue to give attention to them and you will learn to understand them better.

Why Do I Usually Forget My Dreams?

Dreams are usually forgotten because your mind works differently when you sleep than when you are awake. Soon after you awaken, write about your dream. But never worry if you can't remember them at all. If it is important for you to understand your dream, you will remember it. Deep in your mind you will learn something from your dreams even at the times they are not remembered.

Why Do I Have The Same Dreams Over And Over?

If you dream the same dream over and over there is an important message in it for you. Try to find someone who can explain your dream so you can understand what your dream means. Once you understand your dream's message, you will not dream that dream again.

What Does It Mean When What I Dreamed About Happens To Me Later?

Those are dreams that tell you something about what will happen in the future. Those dreams often "look" like your real life so that you can understand them more quickly. They can sometimes be a warning about something you should or should not do. Give attention to this kind of dream and you will understand the message.

Why Do I Sometimes Have Nightmares?

Let me first explain nightmares. A nightmare is a dream that is so frightening that it can awaken you. There are causes for nightmares that I will help you understand.

1. If you have a pain in some part of your body, you may feel this pain while you sleep and it may come into your dream. Sometimes the pain you feel may cause you to scream or cry in your dream.

2. If you eat heavy food before going to bed, your stomach has to work hard to digest the food. If one part of your body is working and another part is resting, it can throw the body off balance and cause restless sleep. If your body is restless, your mind becomes restless and so do your dreams. For a good night's sleep, without nightmares, it is better NOT to eat heavy food before going to bed. Food needs time to digest before you go to sleep.

3. If something has frightened you or you feel sad or angry, you probably will not sleep well because you do not feel peaceful.

So you see, your dreams can be a mirror of how you feel. If you do not feel well, your dreams may not be pleasant. It is important to find out the cause of your nightmares so you no longer will have them.

There is so much to say about dreams that if I were to tell you everything about them, it would fill a whole book. I hope my answers have helped you understand them a little better. Would you like to now awaken and do some exercises?

EXERCISES

Exercise 1: "The Lion"

Bend down on your knees.

Sit on your heels with your back straight.

Place your hands on your knees (look at the picture).

Now open your mouth as wide as you can and stretch every muscle in your face.

Put your tongue out as far as possible so you look as ferocious as a lion. Try to roar.

Stay in this position for a moment so that you can loosen all your tension or tightness.

Close your mouth, take a deep breath, and slowly let it out.

Repeat this exercise and deep breathe once more.

Exercise 2: "The Cat"

Kneel on your knees.

Make your back very straight.

Place both hands flat on the floor with fingers facing forward (look at the pictures).

Now pull your stomach in while you breathe out. Push your back up while your head goes slightly down between your arms (picture A).

Hold to the count of five.

Breathe in while you bring the middle of your back down. Lift your head back up and count to five (picture B).

Repeat all of the exercise five times, very slowly.

Then, sit down and shake your legs and hands.

Relax for a few moments.

A

B

Exercise 3: "Head To Toe"

Sit down and make your back very straight. Stretch your closed legs in front of you.

Bring your feet straight up so that the back of your knees touch the floor.

Bring both arms up and stretch them as high as you can. Keep your head between your arms, looking straight ahead.

Now bring your arms down and reach as far forward as you can without hurting your back (look at the picture).

Try to grab your feet or as far down your legs as you can reach.

Gently bring your chest down to your knees and hold this position to the count of eight.

Slowly come back to the sitting position.

Place your hands in your lap and take two deep breaths.

Shake your hands and wiggle your feet.

Relax a moment and do this exercise again.

A "WALK" INTO YOUR MAGIC GARDEN

Close your eyes. Take three deep breaths. Tighten and then relax every part of your body. (If you don't remember how to do this, read page 12 in Day One again.) Place your arms next to you with your palms facing up.

Watch yourself walking on the path leading to your Magic Garden. Open the gate with your key and close the gate behind you. Walk through your garden and water the grass and the flowers. Spend some time doing whatever you think needs to be done in your garden. (A few moments of silence.) You feel so good doing all those things. You are taking responsibility for your garden. Work can be very pleasant, can't it. Now is a good time to play or to do whatever you enjoy doing in your garden. (A few moments of silence.)

Before you leave your garden, let me explore something with you. Find a nice spot in your garden to sit. Listen to all the sounds around you. Listen to one sound at a time. Really concentrate and become familiar with that sound. (A few moments of silence.) Do you enjoy that single sound? How does it make you feel? Try to become part of that sound. (A moment of silence.)

When you are ready, shut off that sound and listen to a different sound. Try to become part of that sound. How does that sound feel to you? Explore this sound in the same way you did the first sound. Then, if you can, go on to a third sound. When you have explored all the sounds that you can hear, try to remember which one felt best to you. (A few moments of silence.) Why did you like that sound best? Did it make you feel really good? Concentrate on that sound again on other days. As you go along in meditation, you may discover a different sound which makes you feel even better.

Now it is time to leave your Magic Garden. Close the gate and put the key in your pocket. See yourself back in your room. Close your palms and slowly open your eyes. Try to remain quiet and still for a few moments.

Tomorrow I will tell you about feelings. See you then.

DAY FOUR

WHAT ARE FEELINGS?

Hello, my friend! I feel very happy that you have stayed with me in the Magic Garden all this time. Today, I am going to tell you about feelings.

QUESTIONS AND ANSWERS

What Are Feelings?

Feelings are your heart's "answers" to things you see happen around you, to things other people do or say to you, and to experiences you have had. These situations send messages that move about in your heart and cause you to act in certain ways. Those heart "answers" or feelings have names. Some of them are love, joy, anger, and fear. You cannot see or touch feelings. You can only see the expression of feelings. For example, if your friend feels angry, you cannot see or touch his or her anger. But, you will be able to see the expression of that anger in the look on the friend's face or his or her actions. You may even hear anger in the words the friend uses. Feelings and actions usually work together.

Should I Hide Or Just Not Think About Those Feelings?

No, not at all. When those feelings come within you, look at them and try to find out why and from where they came. It is possible to get rid of them in a way that will not hurt you or anyone else. I will tell you about that in a later question.

44

Why Do I Become Angry?

You have those feelings because someone has pushed one of your "sensitive buttons." That means that someone did something which hurts a place inside of you where you don't feel too good about yourself.

Am I Unhappy With Myself Or With The Other Person When I Am Angry?

Most of the time, you feel and express feelings that are coming from inside of you and not from the other person. The other person only helps to show you where you are not happy with yourself. You can say something to one person and it does not bother him or her at all. But if you say that same thing to another person, he or she may get very angry and yell at you. This shows you how everyone reacts to what another person says or does in a different way. You will react to another person depending on how you feel inside about yourself.

How Can I Deal With My Feelings When I Get Blamed For Something I Did Not Do, Or When I Get Punished Unfairly?

We are all mirrors for one another. What you see in other people is usually the reflection or image of your own feelings. The person blames you for something because he or she is angry at himself or herself and not at you. But, he or she does not know this. If you also get angry you will begin fighting with the other person and the throwing of anger between you becomes like a Ping-Pong game. The anger is hit back and forth as you would hit a ball back and forth. You both feel badly and no lesson is learned. Remember in Day One that I told you about the idea how that things that happen to you are meant as lessons from which you can learn more about yourself. You will get hurt until you learn how to handle your feelings well. Try to understand what lesson can be learned from each unpleasant experience and why the other person feels so unhappy. Explain to the other person in a nice way (whenever you are ready) that you can understand that they are angry because you also become angry at times. Tell the person, too, that you really did not do it with the intention of hurting him or her.

How Can I Control My Anger Without Hiding It?

You can control your anger by first taking three deep breaths. Then tense up or tighten your whole body. Make a fist, clench your teeth, and feel every part of your body tightening up. Try to feel like a puppet whose strings are tightly pulled. Then relax as when a puppet's strings all fall free. Feel every muscle in your body let go and feel relaxed. If you still feel some anger, stand before a mirror and watch yourself heave your right fist upwards while saying a long "a" in an angry voice. Then heave your left fist into the air while saying a long "b" with an angry voice. Continue with your right and left fist, using all the alphabet letters, until your anger turns into laughter. As you watch all this in the mirror, you will see how funny it is to watch yourself showing anger.

What Is Fear And Why Am I So Often Afraid?

Fear is a feeling caused by something that makes you act with worry and uneasiness. There are two kinds of fears. There is a good fear which causes you to run away from, or warns you to stay away and to be careful of anything that is truly dangerous and can hurt you. For example, you should fear playing with fire or dangerous tools, running into traffic, or exploring unsafe places. It is important to pay attention to that kind of warning so that you can avoid accidents.

Another fear is the fear that your own mind creates. This fear can feel just as frightening as the other fear. However, it comes from a place deep within yourself where you are not feeling too comfortable. There is no real danger that can be seen by anyone else even though you feel afraid. You see a danger which your mind has made up and it frightens you. Have you ever walked down the street and become afraid as you saw a dog coming towards you? The fear may have caused you to get the chills and become tightened up so that you can't even talk as you pass by the dog. Yet, your friend who is walking with you keeps right on talking. He or she is not at all bothered by the sight of the dog. Your friend may even stop to pet the dog before going on. In your minds, you and your friend have each told yourselves something different about the dog. So can you see how that fear comes from within you and not from the outside? Feelings of fear can happen whether you are a boy or a girl. Everyone is the same within, whether one is a boy or a girl.

How Can I Get Over My Fears?

When you are afraid, try to be still for a few moments. Close your eyes and take a few deep breaths. Try to see or just feel the bright white light within your heart I told you about on Day Two. The light is an inner energy which is so strong that it will always protect you. Once you learn to believe in this inner energy and remember that it is always with you, you will no longer be afraid.

What Is Jealousy And Why Are My Friends Sometimes Jealous Of Me?

Jealousy is a kind of anger toward another person because one feels the other person has something they don't have. Your friends may become jealous of you because they do not think much of themselves. They may not know that they can do everything they want to do if only they will come to believe in themselves. They still need to learn how to feel good about themselves. The only way you can help them is to be very nice to them. You cannot change other people. Others will change as they come to learn their own lessons. But you can help others if you will just love them as they are. You can also let them know the things they do well and when something looks good on them. This will help them to build good feelings about themselves.

Why Do I Get So Frustrated When I Make A Mistake While Playing A Game?

You may feel deeply disappointed (frustrated) because you are playing a game not just for the fun and sport of it but to win or to show off. When you play a game only to win or to show off, you are missing the point or the purpose of a game. The purpose in playing most games is recreation. Another word for recreation is amusement which means having fun. When you play a game because you feel you have to win or

47

show how good you are, the game is no longer for amusement. You are frustrated when you become tense and do not play as well as you had intended to play.

To avoid becoming frustrated, play a game of kickball just because it is fun to kick a ball and run. Forget about winning or showing off and think about what you are doing. Think about the ball and where you want it to go. Then, when you kick it, you will be surprised to find how the ball will follow your directions. You have to be calm and feel good about yourself even in playing a game. Whether you are playing a game of any sort or doing something with your hands such as drawing or playing a musical instrument, it should give you good feelings. If you feel good and enjoy what you are doing, the winning and satisfaction will come naturally.

What Can I Do When Hard Work Or A Test Frustrates Me?

If you become frustrated while taking a test or doing hard work, calm yourself by taking a few deep breaths. For a moment, clear your mind of all thoughts and try to feel good about yourself. Just notice how this will help you to do better in your work or when taking tests.

EXERCISES

Exercise 1: "The Cobra"

Lie face down on the floor and place your arms at your sides with palms of your hands facing up.

With back muscles, raise your chest from the floor and bring your head back (picture A).

Place your hands in front of you so that they are level with your shoulders (picture B).

With your hands, push up very slowly until your back is arched back and your head is drawn back (picture C).

When your arms are totally stretched out and your back is arched as far as it feels good to you (do not force), hold this position and count slowly to ten (picture D).

Now begin to lower your body very slowly in the same way as you moved up.

When your chest has nearly reached the floor, place both arms along side of you on the floor and continue to come down slowly.

As your head reaches the floor, place your cheek on the floor and rest a few moments.

Breathe deeply using slow in and out breaths.

Do "The Cobra" exercise once again.

Remain on the floor for the next exercise.

A

B

C

D

Exercise 2: "The Bow"

Lie on your stomach with your chin touching the floor.

Stretch your arms out away from your body. Bring your legs and feet close together flat on the floor.

Bring your legs back toward your head. Reach back and with your left hand grab your left foot and with your right hand grab your right foot.

Hold them firmly, bring your chest up, and lift your head.

Now try to raise your knees and bring your head back.

Try to hold this position as you count to ten.

While still holding your feet, drop your knees and chin back to the floor.

Let go of your feet, stretch out your legs, and rest your arms along side of you.

Lay your cheek on the floor and rest a few moments.

Feel totally relaxed and repeat "The Bow" exercise once more.

Both of these exercises are very good for strengthening your back.

Exercise 3: "The Complete Breath"

Sit with your legs crossed as in the picture. Hold your back straight and place your hands on your knees.

Breathe in through your nose very slowly.

As you bring in as much air as you can, feel your stomach become larger.

Bring in some more air very slowly through your nose and watch how far your chest expands.

Now hold in the air and slightly raise your shoulders while counting to five.

Very slowly let out all the air through your nose as you lower your shoulders to the normal position and count to ten.

Repeat "The Complete Breath" exercise two more times and you will be ready for your Magic Garden "walk".

Because you just finished a deep breathing exercise, you need only to tense and relax your body before taking your Magic Garden "walk".

A "WALK" INTO YOUR MAGIC GARDEN

Close your eyes and place your arms next to your body with palms up.

See yourself walking on the road leading to your Magic Garden. You are now in front of the gate. Unlock the gate with your key and close the gate behind you.

Walk through your garden and notice the color and good smell of your flowers. Now take time to check all the things that you have to do to keep your garden beautiful. Watch yourself busily taking care of everything. (A few moments of silence.) Do your work slowly and complete each job before going on to another job. Take the time to look over all the work you have done. Do you get that wonderful feeling of a "job well done"? Now that everything looks the way you want it to, take some time off to play in your garden. (A few moments of silence.)

Will you play a little game with me? Watch yourself lying comfortably in the grass. Now think about what is going on inside of your body. Be very still and listen to all the different sounds coming from within your body. How many different sounds can you hear? Take the time to notice each one of them. You may hear sounds you have never noticed before. (A few moments of silence.) Wherever you hear a sound in your body, spend some time exploring that part. Try to block out all other noises so you can listen to that sound really well. Does it always have the same sound or does it change and sound differently at another time? (A few moments of silence.) Do you enjoy these sounds? Listen to these sounds a few moments longer. Remember, those sounds belong to you and they are always with you. You may enjoy listening to them whenever there is some time to be very still and quiet.

We all live with ourselves for so many years, yet we don't really know or listen to our own bodies. When you have finished listening to your body sounds, watch yourself getting up from the grass and walking back through your garden. (A few moments of silence.) As you leave your garden, close and lock the gate. Place the key in your pocket.

Now see yourself back in your room. Close your palms and slowly open your eyes. Remember to remain still for a few moments before going on with the activities of your day.

I have enjoyed being with you. I will see you again tomorrow.

55

DAY FIVE

WHY DO FEELINGS GET HURT?

Hello, my beautiful one! Welcome to our fifth day together. Did I hear a boy just say that he may be handsome but certainly not beautiful? The beauty I am talking about is inner beauty of the Self. The inner Self is not concerned whether you are a boy or a girl. Let me tell you about feelings again today because feelings play such an important part in your life.

QUESTIONS AND ANSWERS

Why Do Feelings Get Hurt?

If someone says no to you, do you think that the person does not love you or understand you? Sometimes you let those thoughts get deep within you so that they hurt your feelings. You do not have to allow that because, as you can see, those feelings just come from your own mind.

For example, you may ask your Mom to drive you to a friend's home for a visit. If she answers that you cannot go today, you may feel hurt and think that she does not care about you. In her mind she cares very much for you. She may have her own reasons for saying no that may have nothing at all to do with you.

Learn to accept 'no' answers without feeling hurt. A slight disappointment is not all that important anyway. Once you understand that, your life will be so much easier for you.

How Can I Keep My Feelings From Becoming Hurt?

First understand that you shouldn't take things too seriously. Life can be fun. Let me explain a pretend game for you to play for a few days. Pretend that you are an actor or an actress in a movie. Try to be both audience and the movie star at the same time. Watch what other people say or do to you and what you say and do to them. What do you think when you watch yourself get all upset and cry or scream? During a quiet moment, ask yourself why you felt so hurt at that part of the movie. Once you can answer that, you may want to discuss it calmly with the person who you believe led you to get upset.

How Can I Keep From Feeling Hurt When My Friends Have Things That My Parents Won't Let Me Have?

First understand that your parents have reasons for not allowing you to have these things. Those reasons may not have anything to do with you. They may have more to do with their own feelings and beliefs about these things.

Suppose you would like to have a cat. You know that most of your friends have pets. But, your parents will not let you have a cat for a pet and you feel hurt. The reason your parents may object to a pet could be because they simply do not feel comfortable with an animal in the house. I am sure that you understand that they could possibly have different feelings about pets than you do. Talk the idea over with them so that you and your parents can understand one another's feelings. That may be the way to find a happy solution for all of you.

Why Am I So Embarrassed When Others Tease Me?

You may experience an upset of self-consciousness because you think the other person doesn't like something about you. When this happens you choose to feel badly. Those upset feelings probably come because you believe that what others think of you is more important than what you think of yourself. If that happens, just remember to look within yourself. Within your heart is a place where you can feel secure, happy, and loved. You can reach into this place whenever you concentrate on your inner light during a quiet moment or while meditating.

Why Do I Feel So Disappointed When I Don't Get What I Want?

Disappointment comes when you don't receive what you had expected. For example, if you go to a bakery to buy a loaf of bread, the salesperson may give you one of those fancy pink and white frosted cookies from the display case. You feel so happy and surprised because you certainly did not expect to receive a free cookie. If you had walked into the bakery expecting to receive one of those big chocolate covered cookies, you would have felt disappointed with the other cookie and not happy at all. When you stop expecting things you will really enjoy what you receive.

Why Is It Important That I Tell The Other Person How I Feel?

It is very important for you to communicate (talk things over) with your family and friends when your feelings get hurt because if you keep your hurt feelings hidden, a feeling of dislike or resentment builds up within you. Resentment is like a water kettle that lets out steam little by little when it boils. If the opening was sealed, the steam could not get out and the kettle would explode. Your feelings work like that. If you keep all your hurt feelings buried inside, they may build up and one day all of your anger may explode. You can build good relationships without resentment if you will let others know how you feel. Then the other persons may also share their feelings with you in an open and friendly manner.

Why Is It Important That I Learn To Listen To Others?

In order to have a good relationship with your family and friends, it is important to listen to them so that you can learn to understand them in the same way you wish to have them understand you. Listen to them to learn about their feelings. This will help build a good relationship with your family and friends that can be a "win-win."

What Is A "Win-Win" Relationship?

A "win-win" relationship is one in which you do things for and with the other person to make him or her feel good; and, the other person does things for and with you that make you feel good. For example, your best friend missed school for a few days. He or she asks if you would explain some of the homework he or she does not understand. You bicycle over to your friend's house and spend time explaining all of the work that he or she missed in school. Your friend is so happy for your help because now he or she can complete the homework. Because you like your friend so much, you felt very happy to help him or her and to give of your time. The "win-win" is the good feeling that each received from the other.

EXERCISES

Exercise 1: "Shoulder Movements"

Sit on the floor and cross your legs. Make your back straight and let your arms relax at your side.

Bend your elbows and turn your palms so that they face you.

Think of where your shoulders meet your arms. That joint can be moved in a circle.

Move that part of your shoulders backward and continue moving it in a circle.

Make eight circles.

Relax a moment.

Now do the same movements in circles going forward.

Exercise 2: "The Neck Roll"

Cross your legs and straighten your back.

Slowly bend your head forward and press your chin against your chest. Close your eyes while counting to five (picture A).

Roll your head slowly to the left as far as you can and hold it there while counting to five (picture B).

Now gently roll your head to the back and feel your chin and throat muscles stretching. Count to five while holding this position (picture C).

Roll your head as far to the right as you can while counting to five (picture D).

Now bring your head to the forward position with your chin resting on your chest. Do this complete exercise three more times.

Try the same exercise but begin it by rolling your head to the right.

"Shoulder Movements" and "The Neck Roll" will help you to relax, especially after sitting all day in the classroom.

A

Exercise 3: "Nostril Breathing"

Get into the same sitting position as for the other two exercises.

Once you have learned how to do this exercise, always close your eyes while doing it.

Make sure your back is straight.

You will be using all the fingers of one hand for this exercise. I will explain the work of each finger as we go along. Be patient and this exercise will soon be very easy for you.

Gently blow the air out of both nostrils so that they feel clear.

Now place your right thumb against your right nostril and place your index and middle finger on your forehead.

Place your ring and little finger close to your left nostril but without touching it.

Push your thumb against the right nostril to close it.

Breathe in very slowly through your open left nostril while counting to four.

Then close your left nostril with your ring finger so that both nostrils are closed.

Hold your breath while counting to four.

Lift your ring finger and very slowly let out the air while counting to eight.

Again, breathe in slowly through your left nostril while counting to four.

Close your left nostril with your ring finger and count to four.

Lift your ring finger and slowly let out the air while counting to eight.

The right nostril remains closed while you open and close your left nostril.

Do this part of the exercise two more times.

Now repeat the exercise with your left hand. Place your left thumb on your left nostril and your index and middle finger on your forehead.

Place your ring finger close to your right nostril without touching it.

Breathe in slowly through your right nostril while counting to four.

Then close the right nostril with your ring finger and count to four.

Now slowly let out the air through your right nostril while counting to eight.

The left nostril remains closed while you breathe in, hold, and breathe out with the right nostril.

Do this part of the exercise two more times.

This exercise is very good for deep breathing. It helps you to relax and also helps to clear your nose which allows more air to come into your lungs. The more air you can get into your body, the better you will feel.

Are you ready to take your Magic Garden "walk"? Since you have already done a deep breathing exercise, you need only to relax your body muscles before going on your "walk".

A "WALK" INTO YOUR MAGIC GARDEN

Close your eyes and relax your arms at your side with your palms up. Now watch yourself on the road leading to your Magic Garden. You are in front of the gate. Open the gate with your key and close the gate behind you.

Walk through your garden and see all the different kinds of flowers and their beautiful colors. Now look at the sky and see how all those colors blend together. Are there any birds singing? Can you hear or see them? (A few moments of silence.)

It's time now to get busy and care for your garden. Watch yourself walking around and doing all the work which needs to be done. (A few moments of silence.) While working and moving about in your garden, you may want to stop here and there to talk to your flowers or to the animals that you may have there. They all can understand you. If you listen carefully, they may even answer you. Take time now to play and to do what you like. (A few moments of silence.)

Now let me show you another game. Find a comfortable grassy spot and lie down. You feel good lying in the soft grass and looking up at the sky. Suddenly you see a large rainbow. Look at all those beautiful colors! Choose one of the colors that you like the best. Watch this color move away from the others and float down towards you. As it comes nearer, you see that it looks like a long strip of soft cloth. Take it into your hands and feel how soft it feels to your touch. Stand up and wrap it all around you. How does it feel to be wrapped up in this color? Does this color make you feel good when you have it wrapped all around you? Now wrap it only around your arms and legs. Does this make you feel any different? (A moment of silence.) Again take the color and wrap it around your body and hair. Does that make you feel happy and put you into a good mood? Play with your color for a little while. (A few moments of silence.)

Think about why you may have picked this color from among all the others. (A few moments of silence.) When you finish playing with your color, send it back into the sky. Watch it take its place among the other colors in the rainbow. (A few moments of silence.) Now walk slowly through your garden to the gate. Walk through the gate, close it behind you, and lock it with your key. Place your key in your pocket.

See yourself back in your room. Close your palms and slowly open your eyes. Remain quiet for a few moments.

Thank you for spending this time with me. I will see you tomorrow.

DAY SIX

HOW DOES THE MIND WORK?

Hello, dear friend. Thank you for joining me again. Today I will tell you about one of your most magic tools, your mind.

QUESTIONS AND ANSWERS

What Are Thoughts?

Thoughts are the mental pictures and ideas that result from your mind at work. Your mind's thoughts can change a lot of things in your life and actually create your own private world. You have total control of your own thoughts. If you think happy thoughts you will feel happy. If you think sad thoughts you will feel sad. If you think frightening thoughts you will feel afraid. I will help you to see how this idea can work for you.

How Can I Have Happy Thoughts When Someone Becomes Angry With Me?

When someone becomes angry with you, there is no rule that says you must also become angry. On Day Four I explained to you how that we are all mirrors for one another. You have come to understand that if someone is angry with you it is because that person does not feel good about himself or herself. You will help the other person and yourself if you send out happy and loving thoughts. Practice this and see if this doesn't happen.

How Can I Think Happy Thoughts When Nothing Seems To Go Right For Me?

You can say to yourself, "All right, this or that happened but it is really not that important." Then begin thinking good thoughts about something you really like. Or, you could take a few deep breaths and go for a "walk" into your Magic Garden. All you need to learn is how not to get upset when things don't go the way you want them to. The more you learn to think happy thoughts at those times, the happier life will be for you.

Can My Mind Help Me To Stay Healthy?

In a way it can because your mind and your body closely work together. To stay healthy it is important to keep your body and mind healthy. Your mind tells your body to get enough exercise, enough sleep, and the proper food. Proper food for your body is good food. Every day it is necessary to feed your body protein such as meat, cheese, eggs, or soya. Your body also needs vitamins, minerals, carbohydrates, and a little fat. It is also important to cut down, or stop eating, "junk foods" which include all those tempting foods that do your body more harm than good. Try to eat less or, better still, stop eating sugar, candy, chocolate, ice cream, cake, pototato chips, and other "junk food" snacks. Instead, try snacking on fresh fruit, dried fruits, nuts, and other healthy foods. These natural foods will help your body instead of harming it. You might like to try a frozen banana. Place the banana in the freezer and when it is frozen, you will find it tastes very much like ice cream. Once you get "hooked" on healthy foods, you may not care for "junk food" ever again. A healthy body helps to make a healthy mind.

How Do I Keep My Mind Healthy?

Your mind stays healthy when it thinks only happy thoughts. When an unhappy thought comes into your mind, think a pleasant or a funny thought. Your body and your mind work together. Unhappy thoughts start up unhappy feelings and bad feelings can hurt your body. If your body is harmed, it will not function or work well. When the body is not functioning properly, you become sick.

Why Do I Get Sick?

Let me help you understand how you become sick by having you think about a garden hose. When you let water into one end of the hose, it will easily flow through all of the hose. If you bend or squeeze the hose, the water has a hard time getting through. If you press it hard enough, the water will be blocked and not be able to get through. Your body functions like that. As I said before, your body and mind work together like one long hose. When you treat your body well by eating properly, exercising, sleeping well, and thinking happy thoughts, you will be healthy because there is good flow throughout your body. Unhappiness, anger, fear, or poor eating and sleeping habits act like a bend in the hose. They build up blocks in your body. When there are too many blocks built up, the body has to work much harder. That kind of hard work easily tires the body so that it breaks down (like a car) and you become sick.

Could I Be Happy All Of The Time If I Learned To Control My Mind And Accept Only Happy Thoughts?

Yes, you could be happier. But, it takes much practice since each of us is tempted all day long to accept unhappy thoughts. Giving attention to bad or fearful things seems to be easier for most people. It is important to give more attention to the good and happy things if you wish to be happy. Looking at and talking about happy things will make you feel good. When you are happy, good things will happen for you. Try to change from thinking bad or sad thoughts to thinking happy thoughts. It will be worth the effort and you will have received a reward.

Turn to page 15 where you drew your picture of the Magic Garden. At the top of the picture there will be the empty space for the sky. Whenever you are able to turn an unhappy thought into a happy thought, place one silver or gold star in

74

the sky (you can either buy a box of silver or gold star stickers or color them in). Everytime an unpleasant situation changes because of your happy thoughts, give yourself two stars. You are the judge who decides when you deserve a star. You may want to reward yourself with the stars in the evening just before going to bed. Always remember how many stars you have earned with good thoughts. After a few months, your sky should shine brightly. I hope you will shine, too.

EXERCISES

Exercise 1: "The Shoulder Stand"

Lie flat on your back with your arms next to you, palms facing down. Feel completely relaxed.

Raise both of your legs and swing them up so that your hips leave the floor.

Place your hands under your hips and slowly push up on them so that your legs can reach as high as they can.

Try to keep your body in a straight line with your legs and hips.

Go very slowly so that you do not force your body. Press your chin against your chest (picture A).

Count slowly to twenty while holding this position.

After you have done this exercise several times, try to add ten or more counts each time until you can hold up your legs to a count of sixty. Never hold the shoulder stand after it becomes uncomfortable.

It is very important that you follow the instructions for coming down from "The Shoulder Stand."

Bring down your arms to the floor with palms facing down.

Bend your knees and very slowly lower your legs (picture B).

Arch your neck back so that your head does not leave the floor.

After your hips are on the floor, very slowly bring your straightened legs to the floor.

Now relax your body completely.

Look over the pictures and check to see if your hands, legs, and hips were in the correct positions.

Remain lying on the floor after doing the shoulder stand for at least one minute.

This exercise can help your blood flow more easily throughout your body.

A

B

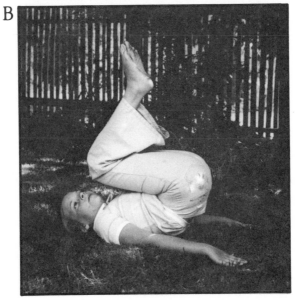

Exercise 2: "Stretching Lying Down"

Lie flat on your back with your arms stretched out behind you.

Point your toes as in the picture.

Now, at the same time, stretch your right arm up and stretch your right leg down.

Then stretch your left arm up and stretch your left leg down in the same way.

Continue stretching your right arm and right leg followed by stretching of your left arm and left leg for twenty stretches.

Bring back your arms along your body.

Next work only with your toes.

Point them forward and count to ten; point them backward and count to ten.

Wiggle your toes for a moment and do this exercise once more.

Now with your arms next to your body work only with your hands.

Make fists with your hands and press them against the floor as you tighten all the muscles in your body.

Count to ten, open your fists, and relax your hands.

Again make fists with your hands and push them against the floor as you count to ten.

Open your fists and relax your hands by wiggling your fingers back and forth.

Take three deep breaths to get you ready for the Magic Garden "walk."

A "WALK" INTO YOUR MAGIC GARDEN

Close your eyes and place your hands next to you with palms up. Watch yourself on the road leading to your Magic Garden. At the gate, open the lock with your key and close the gate behind you.

As you begin walking in your garden among the beautiful flowers, you feel very happy. The flowers smell so good and you really enjoy smelling all the different scents. You have never realized how pleasing it can be to smell so many different flowers.

Now it is time to do all the work that needs to be done. You may also have some animals to feed so take your time. (A few moments of silence.) After you have given your garden all the care it needs, take time to play or do as you please in it. (A few moments of silence.)

Today is a very special day because you are going to receive a gift. As you walk along the path to get to your favorite part of the garden, think about the gift you would most enjoy receiving. The kind of gift I am speaking of could be a special quality such as wanting to become more loving, more happy, or more brave. Or, it could be the development of a special interest such as wanting to be more athletic, more musical, or more artistic. Now you are sitting in your favorite part of the garden, surrounded by beautiful flowers. Take a few more moments to think about the gift you desire. (A few moments of silence.)

Look at one of the yellow flowers very carefully. As the flower slowly opens, out comes a little elf. The elf comes over to you and gracefully bows as it gives you your gift. Hear what the little elf whispers in your ear. It says, "Call on me any time that you like. If you lose your gift, or wish another gift, I can always be found here in this yellow flower. Never forget where I can be found." Watch the elf disappear back into the flower.

Now take a little time and feel your gift becoming a part of you. It is all yours and no one can take it away. Just remember that you have the gift and what it was the little elf told you. (A few moments of silence.)

Walk back through the garden to the gate. After you have left the garden, close the gate and lock it with your key so that no one else can enter your garden.

Now you are back in your room. Close your palms for a few seconds and very slowly open your eyes. Stay very quiet for a few moments.

It feels good to me that I have spent these six days with you. I love you and look forward to seeing you again tomorrow.

DAY SEVEN

HOW CAN LOVE BE SHARED?

My loving friend, I feel so much love for you today that, in my mind, I can see myself giving you a big, warm hug. Today I want to tell you about love.

QUESTIONS AND ANSWERS

How Can I Share My Love?

You can share your love by first loving yourself. If you do not have love for yourself, you don't have love to give away. You cannot share that which you do not have. For example, if you always share your lunch with your friend and one day forget to bring a lunch, you cannot share it even though that's what you want to do. In the same way, you need to have love for yourself before you can share that love with another person.

Is It Selfish To Love Myself?

Loving yourself is not selfish at all if you remember what "loving self" means.

What Does It Mean To Love Myself?

Loving yourself means accepting yourself as a person of value. It means looking within your heart and feeling good about yourself. If you feel good about yourself, you can accept yourself for what you are. If you are a girl, accept being a girl and be really happy about it. If you are a boy, accept being a boy and feel really happy about it. If you are tall or short and heavy or thin, accept yourself for just the way you are.

When you love yourself, you don't become angry with yourself. If your school grades aren't as good as the grades of your friends, love yourself anyway. Within your heart you always know that you did your very best. Knowing that, you will not feel badly because someone else did better than you. If you love yourself, you will always feel good about what you do without having to brag about it.

Loving yourself simply means that you feel happy about yourself and with yourself. It means that you know you always do the best you can. When you are happy and pleased with yourself, you will smile and laugh a lot. Your smiles and laughs will make other people feel good and they will want to be with you.

How Does My Love For Myself Make Other People Feel Good?

It makes others feel good when you share your love. If you feel happy about yourself, you will be much nicer to your family and friends. When you feel good about yourself, the angry feelings or bad moods of others will not much bother you. If you are in a good mood, you will give out good feelings. Good feelings are more catching than bad feelings.

Whenever your parents or friends are in a bad mood, you don't feel good when you are around them. But when they are in a good mood, it makes you happy to be with them. So it is with you. When you are in a good mood, others will feel good being with you.

Why Does My Teacher Always Pick On Me?

Perhaps your teacher picks on you because you are not too happy with yourself. Try to concentrate more on your own schoolwork and don't worry about how well your friends are doing. Listen to your teacher's instruction in class, feel good and loving about yourself and just see what happens.

If Others Pick On Me Or Make Fun Of Me Does That Mean That I Don't Love Myself?

Yes, most of the time that is what it means. A person that is not happy with himself or herself believes deep down that he or she is not a good person. Remember, we are all like mirrors for other people and they can see how you feel about yourself. If you don't feel good about yourself, it becomes very easy for them to pick on or make fun of you. Feeling good about yourself means you can love yourself. If you love yourself, others will feel this and will respect you instead of making fun of you.

Is It True That Animals Can Feel If I Love Or Dislike Them?

Yes, animals are very sensitive or responsive to your inner feelings. Animals are usually very loving creatures and will rarely attack unless they sense you threaten them. Wild animals will attack if they sense danger or are hungry. Do not go near wild animals; they should be left alone because they are not familiar with people. Tame animals or pets can be wonderful friends if you love and care for them.

EXERCISES

Today I will not show you any new exercises. Instead, you may do any of the exercises you wish. You may want to practice all of the exercises, beginning with Day One and ending with Day Six.

Or, you may want to choose only a few to work on.

Always check the written instructions so that you do the exercises correctly.

Perhaps your family or friends would enjoy sharing the exercises and meditation with you.

MEDITATION

Today I would like you to share love in a meditation called "Circle of Love." You may wish to turn on some soft background music. You will join not only me but also Jenny, Lisa, Mark, Tammy, and Tarah who helped me to write this book. You may also like to invite your family and friends to share love with us. Sit in a circle with your legs crossed in front of you and hold hands as we do in the picture. If you are alone, just imagine that you are part of our group. Instead of holding hands, place your palms up as your hands lie on your knees. We will send energy through one hand and receive it through our other hand.

Choose someone in your group to read "Circle of Love" in a slow and soft voice. If you are alone, follow the instructions in Day One for taking the Magic Garden "walk."

CIRCLE OF LOVE

Close your eyes. Breathe in deeply through your nose and blow out slowly through your mouth. (A few seconds of silence.) Again, breathe in deeply through your nose and blow out slowly through your mouth as you would blow out a candle. (A few seconds of silence.) Now picture yourself as a puppet. Imagine every part of your body hanging loosely so that you will get that very relaxed feeling. (About a moment of silence.) Feel any unhappy feelings such as anger, fear, or jealousy leaving you. Watch those feelings slowly disappear into the center of the earth in the same way that water seeps into the ground. (A few moments of silence.)

Now that all the unpleasant feelings have left you, feel the empty space and peace within you. (A few seconds of silence.) Think of a white light shining on top of your head. Watch this light coming into your head and shining throughout your entire body. Feel the warmth and brightness of this light. Feel it flow to every part of your body. (A few moments of silence.) This light is filled with all good feelings such as happiness, peace, joy, and love. These feelings belong to you and they will never leave you. All you must do is remember that they are there. Take of them over and over. The more you take of them, the more they will grow. The more you share them with others, the more their shine will reflect back to you.

Feel all the love you have within yourself. Really feel it move through your body. As you think about that warm feeling of love, send it through your right hand to the person next to you. Because you are all in a circle holding hands, the loving feeling will come back to you through your left hand. Stay very still for a moment as you feel that love leave and return to you.

Now place your hands in your lap with palms face up. Keep your eyes closed and watch yourself walking along the road to your Magic Garden. There is a fence around the garden and you are standing in front of the gate. Reach into your pocket and find the golden key which will open the gate. Enter your Magic Garden for this is your kingdom which has in it anything you want it to have. In your Garden you can do whatever feels good to do. This is your very own special place. Look around to see what it looks like. Is it large and do you see flowers? (A few moments of silence.) Can you hear birds singing? Spend a little time enjoying anything you wish to do in your Magic Garden. (A few moments of silence.) When you are ready to leave, lock the gate and place the key into your pocket. (A moment of silence.)

Close your hands and very slowly open your eyes. Remain still and quiet for a few moments.

Now stand up and form a circle. Stand very close and place your arms around one another. Give everyone a big "Bear Hug." If you are alone, close your eyes and imagine that you are part of the "Bear Hug" circle.

We really love you and we have enjoyed having you in our group. You have become very special to us. It would be so nice to hear from you (check the last paragraph of the introduction which tells you how to do this.)

SHARE A SECRET WITH ME

This may seem to you like the end of this book. I will tell you my secret . . . this book has no end.

Just as you found that each day was a new adventure and a different experience, you may find that each time you go through this book you will understand things differently.

I hope you have enjoyed this book and that you will continue to always enjoy it.

We all send you a big hug and I will look forward to seeing you tomorrow as you and I begin again in Day One.

With much love,
Prabha
(with Jenny, Lisa, Mark, Tammy, and Tarah)